THE
REAL SANTA CLAUS

MARIANNA MAYER

PHYLLIS FOGELMAN BOOKS • NEW YORK

he popular cultural representation of St. Nicholas is based on a combination of more than one country's custom of giving gifts on his feast day. However, the description in "A Visit from St. Nicholas" has played a large part in establishing the modern image of Father Christmas or Santa Claus. Yet how many know the story of the real St. Nicholas? A man of remarkable generosity and kindness, Nicholas is responsible for performing many miracles in his lifetime and after his death some seventeen centuries ago.

A Visit from St. Nicholas

'Twas the night before Christmas, when all through the house
Not a creature was stirring, not even a mouse;
The stockings were hung by the chimney with care,
In hopes that St. Nicholas soon would be there;

The children were nestled all snug in their beds,
While visions of sugar-plums danced in their heads;
And Mama in her kerchief, and I in my cap,
Had just settled our brains for a long winter's nap,

When out on the lawn there arose such a clatter,
I sprang from the bed to see what was the matter.
Away to the window I flew like a flash,
Tore open the shutters and threw up the sash.

The moon on the breast of the new fallen snow
Gave the luster of mid-day to objects below,
When, what to my wondering eyes should appear,
But a miniature sleigh, and eight tiny reindeer,

With a little old driver so lively and quick,
I knew in a moment it must be St. Nick.
More rapid than eagles his coursers they came,
And he whistled, and shouted, and called them by name:

"Now, Dasher! now, Dancer! now, Prancer and Vixen!
On, Comet! on, Cupid! on, Donder and Blitzen!
To the top of the porch! to the top of the wall!
Now dash away! dash away! dash away all!"

As dry leaves that before the wild hurricane fly,
When they meet with an obstacle mount to the sky,
So up to the house-top the coursers they flew,
With the sleigh full of toys, and St. Nicholas too.

And then, in a twinkling, I heard on the roof
The prancing and pawing of each little hoof.
As I drew in my head, and was turning around,
Down the chimney St. Nicholas came with a bound.

He was dressed all in fur, from his head to his foot,
And his clothes were all tarnished with ashes and soot;
A bundle of toys he had flung on his back,
And he looked like a peddler just opening his pack.

His eyes—how they twinkled! his dimples how merry!
His cheeks were like roses, his nose like a cherry!
His droll little mouth was drawn up like a bow,
And the beard of his chin was as white as the snow;

The stump of his pipe he held tight in his teeth,
And the smoke it encircled his head like a wreath;
He had a broad face and a little round belly,
That shook, when he laughed, like a bowlful of jelly.

He was chubby and plump, a right jolly old elf,
And I laughed when I saw him, in spite of myself;
A wink of his eye and a twist of his head,
Soon gave me to know I had nothing to dread;

He spoke not a word, but went straight to his work,
And filled all the stockings; then turned with a jerk,
And laying his finger aside of his nose,
And giving a nod, up the chimney he rose;

He sprang to his sleigh, to his team gave a whistle,
And away they all flew like the down of a thistle.
But I heard him exclaim ere he drove out of sight,
"Happy Christmas to all, and to all a good night."

"A Visit from St. Nicholas" was first published anonymously in 1823, but in 1844 Dr. Clement Moore took credit for penning it,
explaining that he had originally written the poem for his family. However, today scholarly debate casts some doubt as to his authorship.

Long before "A Visit from St. Nicholas" was written, stories of the beloved saint's extraordinary generosity and countless acts of kindness were legendary. Indeed, his very name had become synonymous with the Spirit of Christmas. However, the poem's lively description of St. Nicholas has gone on to shape our modern image of Santa Claus.

Yet sooner or later each of us comes to discover that those longed-for gifts found under the Christmas tree are not after all left by him. But how many of us know that there was a real St. Nicholas?

St. Nicholas lived in Asia Minor around the year A.D. 300 in the city of Myra, a province of Lycia that is today known as Turkey. However, the legends date some 500 years after his lifetime, for long after his death—given as December 6, 343—his bones continued to exude a fragrant healing oil, and reports of his miracles steadily increased. Yet it was the removal of his remains from Myra to Bari, Italy, by a group of Italian merchants and Christian monks in 1087 that seems to have caused the cult of St. Nicholas to spread throughout the West.

Nicholas' reputation as a preserver of ships and sailors resulted in his being honored in seafaring areas such as Holland, Normandy, and the river towns of Germany. The story of his great generosity toward three young girls made him the patron of maidens, and because he was reported to have restored to life three murdered boys, he became the patron of boys as well. By the mid-seventh century, shrines to the saint sprang up all around western Europe.

After the Reformation in the sixteenth century, emphasis on praying to saints was discouraged by both Catholics and Protestants, thus the cult of Nicholas diminished. Nevertheless, traditions and customs of St. Nicholas Day (December 6), such as feasting, St. Nicholas cookies, the giving and exchanging of gifts, survived and traveled with the seventeenth-century Dutch settlers to New York City, known at that time as New Amsterdam.

Then, during the period between the late eighteenth and early nineteenth centuries, New Yorkers of Dutch, German, and English extraction were inspired by the cherished St. Nicholas or Sinter Klaas traditions of Dutch antecedents, and Santa Claus was created. The date of his feast day was fixed to coincide with Christ's birth on December 25, thus St. Nicholas has continued to inspire many throughout the world with the spirit of generosity during the Christmas season.

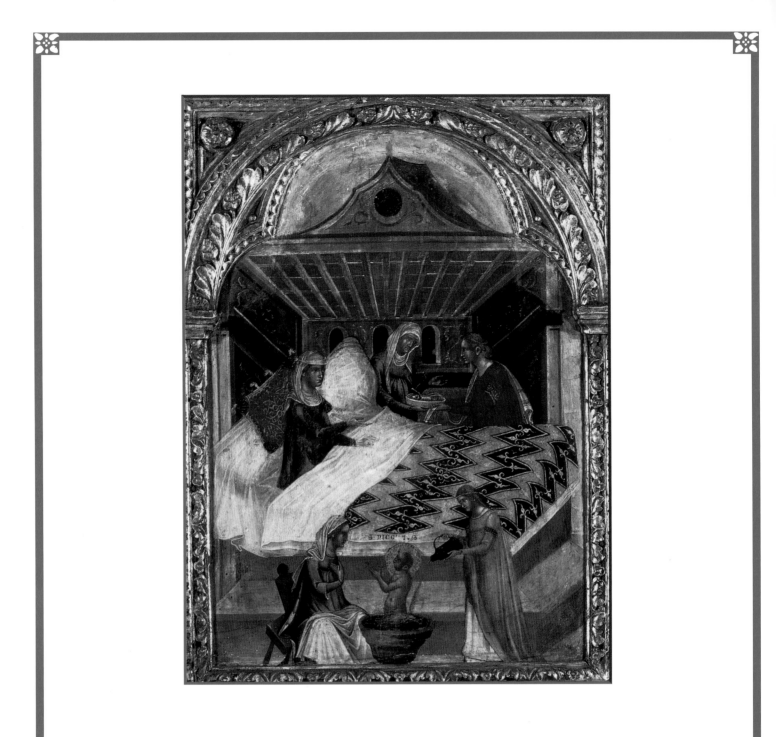

Nicholas' noble parents, Epiphanus and Johanna, were devout Christians, and for many years they prayed for a child. When the Lord blessed them with Nicholas, they were already quite elderly. Sadly, before long, both parents died, leaving the young boy an orphan, but certainly not destitute. Indeed, his parents' estate provided him with a substantial inheritance. Throughout the rest of his life, Nicholas used his wealth to carry out acts of kindness for all those he found in need.

One day while young Nicholas was in the marketplace, he overheard some villagers discussing a once well-to-do neighbor who could no longer provide for his family. Now his three young daughters were to be sold into slavery.

That evening Nicholas lay awake worrying about the family. Finally he crept out in the dead of night and made his way through the dark, empty streets. When he reached the open window of the man's dwelling, he tossed in a bag of gold and then made a hasty retreat.

The next morning the man found the gold, and awoke his daughters to tell them. When a second bag was found the following morning, the man decided to discover the identity of the generous stranger. But how, his daughters wondered, was he to do it?

That night while the rest of the household slept, the man sat and waited by the open window. Hours passed, and his eyelids grew heavy. He tried to keep awake, but soon he fell into a deep sleep. Then the sound of a great thud awakened him. There at his feet lay an even larger bag of gold. Looking out the window, the man saw Nicholas' fleeing figure. "Stop! Stop!" he shouted, and he rushed to follow.

The man was a stronger runner, and he soon overtook Nicholas. Tearfully he embraced his embarrassed benefactor, and begged to know how he might repay him. Nicholas only asked that he promise never to reveal who had helped him.

Thanks to the gold Nicholas had given, the needs of the family were met, and the man's three daughters were provided generous dowries so that they were able to make excellent marriages.

hen the elderly bishop in the city of Myra died, all the church fathers gathered to choose a successor. Among them was a devout bishop of high rank. Hoping that the Lord would guide him in his choice, he went to the church alone to pray. There an angel appeared to him, and said, "Tomorrow at ten o'clock a young man called Nicholas will enter through the gates of the church. He should be the next Bishop of Myra."

In the morning the bishop told his colleagues about the angel, and together they went outside the church to wait. At the stroke of ten, just as the angel predicted, Nicholas entered through the church gates.

Immediately the bishops went and asked his name. When Nicholas told them, they gave thanks to the Lord, declaring his arrival a miracle. Then they led Nicholas into the church and ordained him Bishop of Myra.

A few years after Nicholas was ordained bishop, a man who kept an inn on the outskirts of the city murdered three youths and then hid them in a tub of brine. The innkeeper never expected to be found out, but one night an angel of the Lord appeared to Nicholas and instructed him to visit the inn.

The very next day Nicholas traveled there, though upon entering, he noticed nothing amiss. But divine guidance led him to the tub of brine, and when Nicholas made the sign of the cross over it, the three victims stood up, miraculously restored to life.

Seeing he was discovered, the guilty innkeeper tried to flee. But he was promptly seized and punished. Meanwhile the youths were joyously reunited with their families, and ever after Nicholas has been hailed the patron of young boys.

Micans da nicola
us pontificali de
coratus infula
omnibus se amabilem exhi

Once, a terrible famine swept through the province. Severe drought reaped spare crops, causing storehouses once filled with grain to be quickly exhausted. Now rich and poor alike went hungry. The province faced certain starvation before the long winter ended and new crops could be planted and harvested. Nicholas prayed for a means to deliver his congregation, but it seemed many would die.

Then one frosty morning cargo ships loaded with grain came into port. Nicholas went directly to the ship captains, and begged that a mere one hundred bales of grain be released to the local people.

But the ship captains refused, saying, "Holy father, though we would gladly help, we dare not. The emperor has had our shipments carefully measured and the amounts recorded. If we fail to deliver the exact total to his storehouses in Alexandria, death will be our penalty."

Nicholas would not give up. "Do what I ask," he pleaded. "And when your shipments arrive in Alexandria, our merciful Lord will see that not one kernel of grain will be found missing."

Their hearts went out to the holy man. Though it might mean their deaths, the ship captains agreed. Yet just as Nicholas had promised, when the cargo ships docked at the port in Alexandria, the exact measure of grain was delivered in its entirety.

At the same time Nicholas distributed the gift of grain to each family according to its needs. Miraculously there was more than had been given; indeed, there was enough for more than two years to live on and to plant.

In the seaside province of Myra, Nicholas was known to every sailor and sea captain. He blessed their ships as well as their fishing nets, praying for their safe and bountiful return. It was believed that not a single crewman in the province would set out to sea without a prayer said on his behalf by this good bishop. But blessings or not, the waters of the ocean can be treacherous, and many a good sailor has lost his life though he be skilled and his ship true.

One stormy night, a sudden gale blew up without warning, threatening to engulf a sailing ship and its crew off the coast of Lycia. Violent waves rose high above the ship, winds ripped the sails, and the ship's mast broke with a horrible crack. The ship was flung like a helpless toy upon the turbulent waters. Giving themselves up for lost, each sailor made his peace with the Lord, forsaking all hope of seeing family or loved ones ever again.

But above the roar of the howling winds one sailor stood up and shouted to the others, "We must call upon good Father Nicholas. Let us ask him to intercede with the Almighty to save us!" Turning their back to the rain and the wind, the crew knelt down and prayed: "Holy Father Nicholas, friend of sailors and seafaring ships, we beg you to ask the Lord to help us in our hour of desperate need."

All at once the storm died, and the sea turned perfectly calm. The crewmen scarcely believed their eyes as the dark clouds parted, revealing blue sky and brilliant sunshine. And there high up in the heavens for all to see was the figure of their beloved Nicholas. Even without sails or mast, the vessel navigated homeward. Once they arrived, the sailors swore that it was Nicholas alone who led them safely to port.

Three princes, Nepotian, Ursus, and Apilion, along with their army were sent by Emperor Constantine to put down a rebellion. But once en route, a storm sent their ship instead to the port of Myra. As bishop of the city, Nicholas welcomed them and invited the three princes to his home while they awaited fair weather.

Meanwhile a Roman consul in the city was secretly paid a bribe to have three innocent soldiers beheaded. Nicholas learned of this and, accompanied by his guests, he hastened to the execution. When he burst upon the scene, the condemned men were already on their knees. Blindfolds covered their eyes, and the executioner's sword hung poised above their heads ready to strike. In a flash Nicholas snatched away the sword. Then he untied the men and placed them under his protection.

Next Nicholas and the three princes arrived at the consul's office, where Nicholas forced open the locked door and seized the consul. Shaking the official vigorously, he shouted, "How dare you misuse your authority to condemn innocent men!"

The terrified consul pleaded for mercy and, seeing his genuine repentance, the princes spoke on his behalf. At last Nicholas gave his forgiveness, whereupon the consul swore to make amends to the men he had wronged.

Days later the three princes resumed their journey. After swiftly completing their mission without bloodshed, they went to report to the emperor. Constantine was delighted at the news, and rewarded each handsomely. But jealous courtiers plotted against them, and soon bribed the imperial prefect to falsely accuse all three of treason. The emperor came to believe the lie. He promptly ordered the princes jailed, and sentenced to death without trial.

In despair the condemned men wept bitterly. But Nepotian reminded the others of good Father Nicholas. Hadn't he saved three innocent men only lately, and in their very presence? Perhaps he could help them; it was their only hope. Together they prayed, begging the Lord to send Nicholas to help them.

That night in a dream the figure of an old man appeared to Emperor Constantine. "Blind and stupid man, you have condemned your three most loyal princes for crimes they did not commit. Get up at once and order their release!" demanded the old fellow. "Or I shall pray to God to stir up a terrible war that will bring down your kingdom."

"Who are you," asked the indignant Constantine, "to dare come into the royal bedchamber and threaten the Imperial Emperor of Rome?"

"I am Nicholas, Bishop of Myra," the apparition replied, and then vanished.

That night the same figure appeared to the guilty prefect and said, "Fool! Why did you agree to the killing of three innocent men? Go and set them free. If you don't, your torment will never end and a plague shall be upon your house."

Mustering up his courage, the terrified prefect cried, "I will not be bullied. Who are you?"

"I am Nicholas, Bishop of Myra," answered the vision, and then the prefect awoke.

Truly shaken, both the emperor and the prefect dashed from their beds and each told the other of his dream. Then together they hurried to the prisoners. In a fury the emperor confronted them. "Are you sorcerers with power to delude me with false visions?"

The men fell on their knees, swearing they were innocent, and did not deserve to be killed. Finally the emperor asked if they knew someone named Nicholas. At this the men raised their hands to heaven and gave thanks to God. Constantine demanded they explain, and when they did, he became convinced that it was Nicholas who had come in a dream to speak to him.

At last he said, "You may go free, and give thanks to God for saving you." Then, after a moment's pause, he added, "And tomorrow go to Nicholas of Myra with gifts from me. Ask him please not to threaten me anymore. Instead beseech him to pray for me so that I may never be fooled by lies again."

Now a time came when the Lord called upon his angels to accompany Nicholas to the kingdom of heaven, for the holy man's earthly life was at an end. Nicholas smiled when he saw the angels approaching, and bowing his head, he recited these words: "Into your hands, O Lord, I commend my spirit." Then as a heavenly choir sang out, Nicholas rose with the angels to join the Lord.

After his death St. Nicholas was buried in a marble tomb, and soon a miraculous fountain of oil began to flow from that spot. Then, when the city of Myra fell into the hands of the Saracens, a group brought his remains to Bari, Italy. A new church was built to house his tomb, and to this day a holy oil that is said to restore the sick to good health flows at the site.

Et comme ce fust signe de grant mal et
se ce signe fu comme ce fu grant mal et auss̄
tente se ce ne fu signe

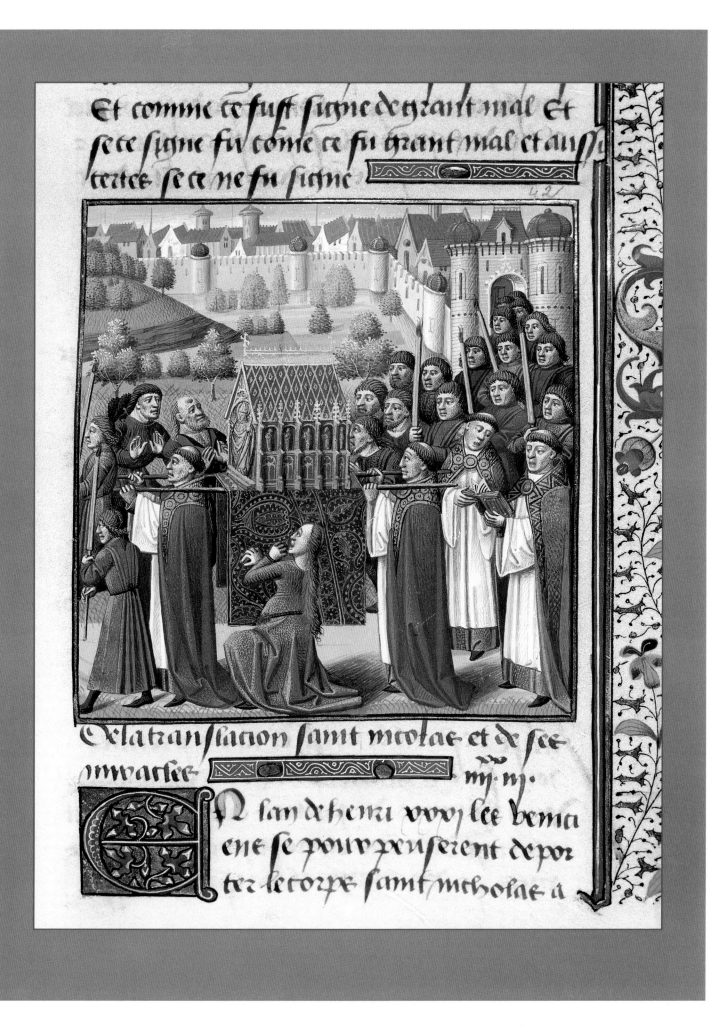

Ou la translation saint nicolae et de sce
mrvartes   iiij. ij.

En l'an d'henri vroy lee venia
ene se pourpenserent depor
ter le corpz saint nicholae a

any wondrous miracles took place in Nicholas' name after his death. At one time a wealthy couple implored the saint to intercede with the Lord so that they might be granted a child. A boy was finally born to them on the feast day of St. Nicholas, and the child was named Adeodatus. In gratitude the parents built a beautiful chapel next to their home. Every Sunday, mass was celebrated, and on St. Nicholas' feast day special prayers were offered and a great party given by the family in his honor.

Then, at the age of nine, Adeodatus disappeared. Though his parents had no way of knowing what had befallen him, they sincerely believed he would one day be restored to them. The following year they celebrated the feast of St. Nicholas as usual, and asked the saint to look after their boy.

Now, the family estate bordered a land inhabited by a hostile people, and it was they who had taken Adeodatus. The boy was made a servant to their king and, though treated moderately well, he bitterly missed his parents. When the feast day of St. Nicholas arrived, Adeodatus' eyes filled with tears as he thought of the wonderful celebration the family was no doubt holding to honor the beloved saint.

The king, observing the boy's distress, demanded to know the reason. But when told, he only laughed, and said, "Stop your tears and forget such nonsense. Your Nicholas has no power in my domain."

Suddenly a great rumbling shook the very floor beneath their feet, and a furious whirlwind blew into the king's palace. The walls crumbled, and as the roof collapsed, another mighty gust snatched the boy and swept him from the ruin.

The next moment the child was deposited safe and sound at the threshold of his parents' chapel. With tears of joy mother and father embraced him, giving thanks to God and St. Nicholas for the return of their son.

A basilica was built in St. Nicholas' honor at Constantinople, and still other churches dedicated to his name can be found overlooking the sea where they were constructed as landmarks for ships and seafarers. Today St. Nicholas continues to remain the patron of sailors. He is also the patron of children, brides and unmarried women, pawnbrokers, perfumiers (because his relics in Bari are said to emit the fragrant scent of myrrh), travelers, pilgrims and safe journeys, Russia, Greece, Sicily, Lorraine, and Apulia.

Saint Nicholas' symbols are the bishop's crosier, three money bags, and a ship's anchor.

A NOTE ABOUT THIS BOOK

Many of us can remember our disappointment to learn that there wasn't a real Santa Claus. My mother revealed the awful truth one morning in September as I was pulling up my socks for my first day at primary school. Stunned, I asked, "Does that mean there isn't an Easter Bunny either!?"

All these years later I embarked on a study of the life of St. Nicholas, the real Santa Claus, with a great deal of curiosity. Discovering the stories surrounding St. Nicholas confirmed a conviction I had long held as a child that such a wonderful character couldn't possibly be mere fiction.

It is very easy to see how Nicholas' generosity won him legions of devoted followers during his life and long after. What better saint to be the model and inspiration for the Spirit of Christmas. Painters over the centuries were captivated by him, particularly those painting during the fourteenth and fifteenth centuries—two of the many periods in history that enjoyed a resurgence of his popularity. However, many artists throughout the centuries devoted themselves to depicting scenes from his legendary life. Thanks to all of them, I was hard-pressed to choose from among so many fine works of art.

Additionally, to bridge the gap between the

legendary man and our rosy-cheeked Santa, I have included images from the late ninteenth century. While coinciding with the first publication of the poem "A Visit from St. Nicholas," the late 1800's and early 1900's marked a time when the commercialization of Christmas had yet to take strong hold of the holy day. Viewing the reverential and the secular images side by side allows an opportunity to pictorially trace the complex evolution of St. Nicholas into Santa Claus from his earliest beginnings to present day. Perhaps the tales and corresponding art can give a glimpse into who the real Santa Claus was and how he might have really looked.

As for my childhood conviction that Santa Claus is more than fiction: The compelling evidence of his generosity supplied by history, legend, and art portrays for me a simple true-to-life human being with a fineness of character that both reflects and encourages the generosity we are all capable of, regardless of the season. And, so long as my faith in him remains, I shall believe that this very real Santa Claus will speak forever to the childlike wonder within us all during the most delightful of holidays.

List of Sources

de Voragine, Jacobus. *The Golden Legends, Volume I.* Translated by William Granger Ryan. Princeton: Princeton University Press, 1993.

Duchet-Suchaux, Gaston, and Michel Pastoureau. *The Bible and the Saints.* Paris/New York: Flammarion, 1994.

McNeill, John. *Illustrated Lives of the Saints.* New York/Avenel, New Jersey: Crescent Books, 1995.

White, Kristin E., comp. *A Guide to the Saints.* New York: Ivy Books, 1991.

List of Illustrations

Nostalgia Cards. Best Christmas Wishes. (SuperStock, FL), front jacket art.

Andrea del Sarto (1486–1530). The Assumption of Mary, detail showing St. Nicholas of Myra with three golden balls (altarpiece). Florence, Italy: Palazzo Pitti (Bridgeman Art Library, NY), back jacket art.

Nostalgia Cards. Santa With Two Angels and His Sleigh. (SuperStock, FL), title page.

Nostalgia Cards. Christmas Greetings: Santa. (SuperStock, FL), page 3.

Jacopo Tintoretto (1518–1594). St. Nicholas of Bari. Vienna, Austria: Kunsthistorisches Museum (Erich Lessing/Art Resource, NY), page 5.

Paolo Veneziano (c.1300–1362). The Birth of St. Nicholas. Florence, Italy: Galleria degli Uffizi (Bridgeman Art Library, NY), page 6.

Gentile da Fabriano (1385–1427). Polittico Quaratesi: Birth of St. Nicholas of Bari. Vatican State: Pinacoteca, Vatican Museums (Scala/Art Resource, NY), page 7.

Ambrogio Lorenzetti (1285–1348). The Charity of St. Nicholas of Bari. Paris, France: Musee du Louvre (SuperStock, FL), page 8.

Hermen Rode (c.1468–1504). Scenes from the Life of St. Nicholas from the Inner Section of the Left Exterior Wing of the Former Main Altar in St. Nicholas's Church, 1481 (tempera on panel). Tallinn, Estonia: Estonian Art Museum (Bridgeman Art Library, NY), page 9.

Irina Ilina. Angel of Happiness (1995). (The Grand Design/SuperStock, FL), page 10.

Hermen Rode (c.1468–1504). Scenes from the Life of St. Nicholas from the Inner Section of the Left Exterior Wing of the Former Main Altar in St. Nicholas's Church, 1481 (tempera on panel). Tallinn, Estonia: Estonian Art Museum (Bridgeman Art Library, NY), page 11.

Lorenzo Veneziano (fl.1356–1379). St. Nicholas and St. John the Baptist. Venice, Italy: Accademia (Cameraphoto/Art Resource, NY), page 12.

St. Nicholas and Three Boys in a Tub. Suffrage to St. Nicholas. Hours of Margaret de Foix. Ms. 2385–1910, fol. 208r. France, 1470–1480. London, Great Britain: Victoria & Albert Museum (Victoria & Albert Museum/Art Resource, NY), page 13.

Pacino di Buonaguida (fl.1303–1339). St. Nicholas of Myra (tempera on panel). Florence, Italy: Galleria dell'Accademia (Bridgeman Art Library, NY), page 14.

Ambrogio Lorenzetti (1319–1374). Detail of the legend of St. Nicholas of Bari: the famine at Myra. Florence, Italy: Uffizi (Nimatallah/Art Resource, NY), page 15.

Fra Angelico (1387–1455). Meeting of St. Nicholas with the imperial messenger and the salvage of the ship with grain. From the predella of the Perugia triptych. Vatican State: Pinacoteca, Vatican Museums (Scala/Art Resource, NY), page 16.

Gentile da Fabriano (1385–1427). St. Nicholas calms the storm (The Quaratesi polyptych). Vatican State: Pinacoteca, Vatican Museums (Scala/Art Resource, NY), page 17.

Anonymous, fourteenth century. St. Nicholas forgiving the consul (fresco). Lower Church, S. Francesco, Assisi, Italy (Scala/Art Resource, NY), page 18.

Hermen Rode (c.1468–1504). Scenes from the Life of St. Nicholas from the Inner Section of the Left Exterior Wing of the Former Main Altar in St. Nicholas's Church, 1481 (tempera on panel). Tallinn, Estonia: Estonian Art Museum (Bridgeman Art Library, NY), page 19.

Hermen Rode (c.1468–1504). Scenes from the Life of St. Nicholas from the Inner Section of the Left Exterior Wing of the Former Main Altar in St. Nicholas's Church, 1481 (tempera on panel). Tallinn, Estonia: Estonian Art Museum (Bridgeman Art Library, NY), page 20.

Anonymous, fourteenth century. St. Nicholas Appearing to Constantine the Great (fresco). Lower Church, S. Francesco, Assisi, Italy (Scala/Art Resource, NY), page 21.

Fra Angelico (1387–1455). St. Nicholas of Bari, death of the Saint. Predella from the Polyptych of the Dominicans, 1437. Perugia, Italy: Galleria Nazionale dell'Umbria (Scala/Art Resource, NY), page 22.

Translation of the relics of St. Nicholas, from Vincent de Beauvais' "Le Miroir Historial."
France, 1470–1480. Ms. 722/1196, fol. 176r. Chantilly, France: Musee Conde (Giraudon/Art
Resource, NY), page 23.

Giotto di Bondone (c.1266–1337). St. Nicholas, from the St. Reparata Polyptych (far right panel
reverse). Florence, Italy: Duomo (Bridgeman Art Library, NY), page 24.

Anonymous, fourteenth century. St. Nicholas liberating Adeodatus and returning a drowned
boy to his family (fresco). Lower Church, S. Francesco, Assisi, Italy (Scala/Art
Resource, NY), page 25.

Lorenzo Lotto (c.1480–1556). St. Nicholas in Glory with Saints. Venice, Italy: Santa
Maria del Carmine (Bridgeman Art Library, NY), page 26.

Carlo Crivelli (c.1430/35–1495). St. Nicholas and St. Michael, detail from San Martino polyptych
(tempera on panel). San Martino, Monte San Martino, Italy (Bridgeman Art Library, NY),
page 28.

ACKNOWLEDGMENTS

Sincerest thanks to Michael Chelminski for suggesting St. Nicholas as a subject one frosty
Christmas day. His additional input once the paintings were selected aided in narrowing down
two tough choices for this book.

Special thanks also to my editor and publisher Phyllis Fogelman for her faith in worthy and
unusual books. Her enthusiasm as always is a constant source of inspiration. And to assistant
editor Rebecca Waugh, who may have come to this project a novice but who has concluded it a
veteran, having assisted me throughout the sorting of the myriad details involved in putting the
book together.

And thanks to Pam Redmer at Design to Printing for refining and in some cases re-creating
the more complex decorative elements within the book. My sincerest gratitude as well to Atha
Tehon and her very able art department for graciously striving to carry through my particular
vision for the final book.

For Michael Chelminski, gifted artist, excellent friend,
and the inspiration for this book

Published by Phyllis Fogelman Books
An imprint of Penguin Putnam Books for Young Readers
345 Hudson Street
New York, New York 10014

Designed by Marianna Mayer
Text set in Centaur
Printed in Hong Kong on acid-free paper

1 3 5 7 9 10 8 6 4 2

Library of Congress Cataloging-in-Publication Data
The real Santa Claus / Marianna Mayer.
p. cm.
Includes bibliographical references.
ISBN 0-8037-2624-4
I. Santa Claus—History—Juvenile literature. [I. Santa Claus. 2. Nicholas, Saint, Bp. of Myra.] I. Title.
GT4985 .M38 2001
384.2663—dc21   00-063610